Dedication

For my wonderful son Sam

And his beautiful Mum Su who is with the stars watching over us

Without the two of you the chicken would never have hatched

– C.C.

Funky Chicken: A Bushy Tale of Crocs and Chooks
© Chris Collin and Megan Kitchin 2012
First published in Australia in 2013 by Funkybooks
PO Box 1933 Hervey Bay Qld 4655 Australia
www.funkybooks.com.au

Book layout and design: Monique Lisbon, Mono Unlimited (www.monounlimited.com)

National Library of Australia Cataloguing-in-Publication entry:

Author:	Collin, Chris E.
Title:	Funky chicken : a bushy tale of crocs and chooks / Chris Collin; illustrated by Megan Kitchin
ISBN:	978-0-9874507-0-8 (Hbk + CD-Rom)
Target Audience:	For primary school age
Subjects:	Animals – Australia – Juvenile fiction
Other Authors/Contributors:	Kitchin, Megan
Dewey Number:	A823.4

This Funkybook
belongs to

_____

Funky Chicken

A Bushy Tale of
Crocs and Chooks

WARNING!

MAY CAUSE UNCONTROLLABLE FITS OF LAUGHTER!

by Chris Collin

Illustrated by Megan Kitchin

A long time ago when the world wasn't old,
Bush animals gathered ... or so it is told.
A meeting was held that went on for a week,
To decide who amongst them was the most unique.

They argued through daylight until it was late,
They chose from all animals, enemy and mate.
In seven long days of ferocious debate,
They picked their contenders ...
of whom there were eight.

Kookaburra who laughed
all day from up high ...

A black cockatoo with a piercing cry ...

The burrowing wombat who lived in a log ...

A beautiful slippery green tree frog ...

The dangerous dingo
with a teeth-gnashing bite ...

The bulgy-eyed possum
who came out at night ...

... And a sneaky old croc
who would give you a fright!

After the animals had all had their say
And the sun went to bed on that seventh day,
The most unique creature of both great and small,
Far from minute – although not very tall,

The rarest,
     the strangest,
          the weirdest of all ...

Was rare Funky Chicken ...

with a very odd call.

"It's barely been seen though!"
the kookaburra cried
And Cockatoo said,
"I'm sure the last one has died!"

The wombat was shaking his head in surprise;
He couldn't believe Funky Chook won the prize.
The tree frog just frowned as she said, "This is silly"
And leapt in the water from off a big lily.

Bulgy-eyed Possum
(who rarely ever spoke),
Said, "Good on ya, Chicken,
you're not a bad bloke!"

The dingo just howled and ran off in the night,
In grave, mortal fear of the crocodile's bite.

But Dingo did not need to worry or stress;
At that time the crocodile couldn't care less.
Old Croc wasn't hungry; he'd eaten before ...
He'd snacked on a bush pig at quarter past four.

He had a good look though – a long sneaky stare,
At that strange little creature standing up there,
Clucking and prancing and strutting around,
The King of Uniqueness – just newly crowned.

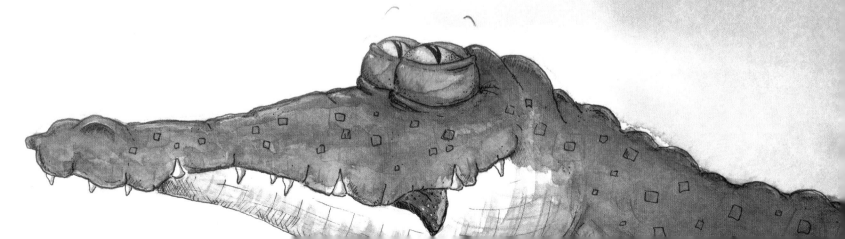

And Croc began thinking,
I wonder, I do –
If Funky Chook tastes
like grey kangaroo ...

Or would he be more
like a black cockatoo?
One thing was for sure though;
the taste would be new.

He had one last thought,
slinking off in the night ...
To munch on that chook
would be such a delight.

Next morning the animals woke up at dawn
To a clamour that gave them no time to yawn.
That chicken was strutting around like a FREAK –
Yelling, "I'm FUNKY CHICKEN. The most unique!"

The animals stared,
Not knowing what to do!
They couldn't believe all this hullabaloo!
Maybe this chicken was best off in a stew!

Kookaburra laughed saying, "What a strange fellow."
The cockatoo said, "He does seem a bit shallow!"
The wombat just couldn't believe his own eyes;
The chook was so loud for a thing of its size!

The tree frog said, "Funky Chook is not cool!
This jibber and jabber! He looks like a fool!"
The nocturnal possum just went off to sleep,
High up in his tree in a small furry heap.

Then Dingo howled out,
"Bring the chook over here!
My breakfast can start
With a chunk of its ear!"

That chook didn't listen to what they were saying.
All day he went on with his bragging and braying:
"Funky Chicken is best! Funky Chicken is great!
The coolest animal in all of the states!"

The clamour went on
For the rest of that day.
By night time they all wished
He'd just go away!

There was one among them who wished him to stay;
Old Croc had been watching him closely all day.
Croc didn't care about old Dingo Dog,
Or Burrowing Wombat who lived in a log.

Old Croc – he had other ideas on that night;
He only had one creature set in his sight.
The one thing that night
That kept his lips lickin' ...

Yes, sneaky Old Croc tried
to EAT Funky Chicken!

Although you now know funky chooks aren't too smart
They move very quickly when given a start ...
And with Lady Luck by his side on that day,
The croc missed his mark and the chook got away!

"You can't eat me, Croc –
I'm far too unique!"
And he ran and he ran
For the rest of that week.

Humpty Doo

He ended up somewhere beyond Humpty Doo,
On an egg farm with Bob and his lovely wife Sue.
There he wound up with some chooks in a pen
And the bush never saw Funky Chicken again!

The one thing the animals learnt on that night
(Other than crocs might eat chooks in one bite) ...
Whilst it's nice to be famous just once in a while
And strut 'round the bush with an "I'm famous" smile

Sometimes it's best
to take a lower profile ...

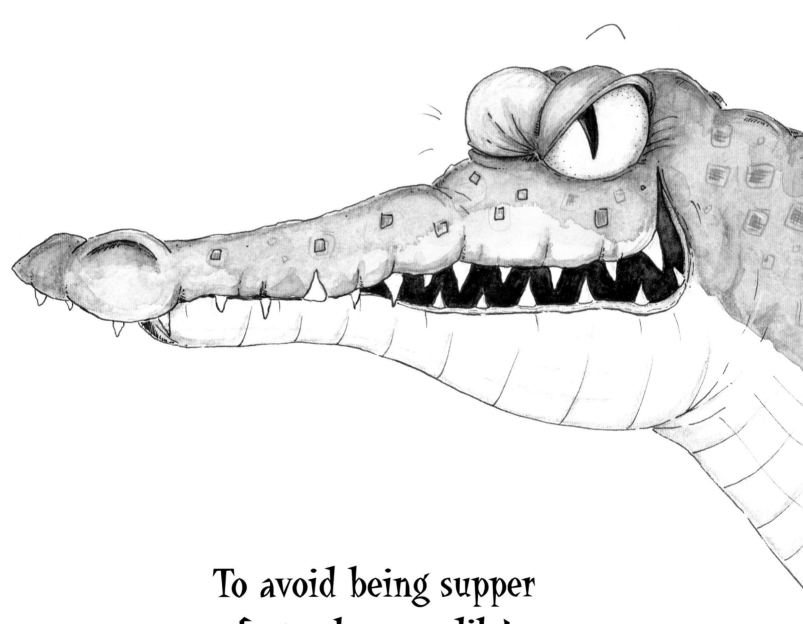

To avoid being supper
for a sly crocodile!

Chris Collin (Author)

Chris has been writing for a number of years and made the decision in 2012 to publish his stories and become a full-time writer of children's books.

His aim is to bring laughter, joy and general funkiness into children's lives, whoever and wherever they are!

Funky Chicken: A Bushy Tale of Crocs and Chooks is his first book.

Megan Kitchin (Illustrator)

Megan has always loved illustrating. She completed a Bachelor of Graphic Design and then went on to travel and nanny overseas.

After her return to Australia she decided she really enjoyed working with children, so went on to become a teacher. This was a great decision as it has enabled her to combine the two things she loves most ... drawing and children.

To date she has worked as an art teacher and is currently applying her creativity in her work at a kindergarten.

Megan is super-excited to be illustrating *Funky Chicken*. Illustrating children's books is something she has always planned to do ... and what a great little character to begin with!

We're lending a hand!

Funkybooks is committed to helping kids who may need a little more funkiness in their lives.

A donation for every book sold through our website will go towards organisations who aim to enhance the lives of children and their families. See www.funkybooks.com.au for more information on this and other ways we can all help to make the world a funkier place!